One Humpy Grumpy Camel
published by
Stacey International
128 Kensington Church Street
London W8 4BH
Tel: 020 7221 7166; fax: 020 7792 9288
Email: marketing@stacey-international.co.uk
www.stacey-international.co.uk

ISBN: 1 900988 755

CIP Data: A catalogue record for this book is available from the British Library

© Julia Johnson & Emily Styles 2003
Reprinted 2005

3 5 7 9 0 8 6 4 2

For William

Design: Sam Crooks

Printing & Binding: SNP Leefung, China

1 One Humpy Grumpy Camel

Written by Julia Johnson

Illustrated by Emily Styles

STACEY INTERNATIONAL

It is dawn in the desert,
See the rising sun,
Everything is stirring
And the day has just begun.

1

One humpy grumpy camel
Sets off across the land,
In search of all his friends –
He follows footprints in the sand.

4

Two little Fennec foxes
Raise their heads and look around.
Can you see what they can see
Hopping along the ground?

3

Three long-eared hares
Do not dare to stay.
With strong back legs and clouds of sand
They quickly leap away.

 Four sharp-eyed falcons
Flying way up high
Have seen the leaping hares
And swoop down from the sky!

5

Five silly billy goats
Munching cardboard boxes –
They're far too busy eating
To notice the little foxes!

9

6

Six tired donkeys
Laden down with sacks –
Dates and rice and coffee
Are strapped upon their backs.

Seven sunning lizards
Blink their hooded eyes,
A quick flick of their tongues
And they've gobbled up some flies!

11

Eight baby scorpions
Climb up on to their mother.
They take a ride perched on her back
Squeezed one next to the other.

Nine busy beetles
Roll their balls of dung
And pop them into little holes
So they can feed their young.

10

Ten leafy palm trees –
There must be water near.
Come to the oasis,
It's cool and shady here.

Eleven crested hoopoes –
Do you hear what they say?
It's a message for our camel
To help him on his way.

11

Twelve buzzing bees
Busy making honey,
We all like to eat it –
Sticky, sweet and runny!

13

Thirteen wise old men
Telling stories in the shade.
Fingering their prayer beads,
They watch the daylight fade.

14

Fourteen pretty dancing girls
Swing their long black hair.
See their jingling bangles
And the coloured robes they wear.

Fifteen china coffee cups
Laid out upon a tray
To make a traveller welcome
In the old Arabian way.

Sixteen Bedouin ladies
Busy with their cooking,
Dipping in their fingers
When no-one else is looking!

16

Seventeen incense burners
With perfumes rich and rare
Are passed from guest to guest,
Their fragrance fills the air.

Eighteen glowing lanterns
Shine out across the night
Lighting up the tent –
Now there's a lovely sight!

Nineteen naughty boys
Take a peep inside,
And there upon a cushion
Sits a beautiful young bride.

20

Twenty smiling camels
Look up to see their friend,
And he's no longer grumpy
Now his journey's at an end!

It is night in the desert
And there's a wedding feast
And everyone's invited –
Each girl and boy and beast.

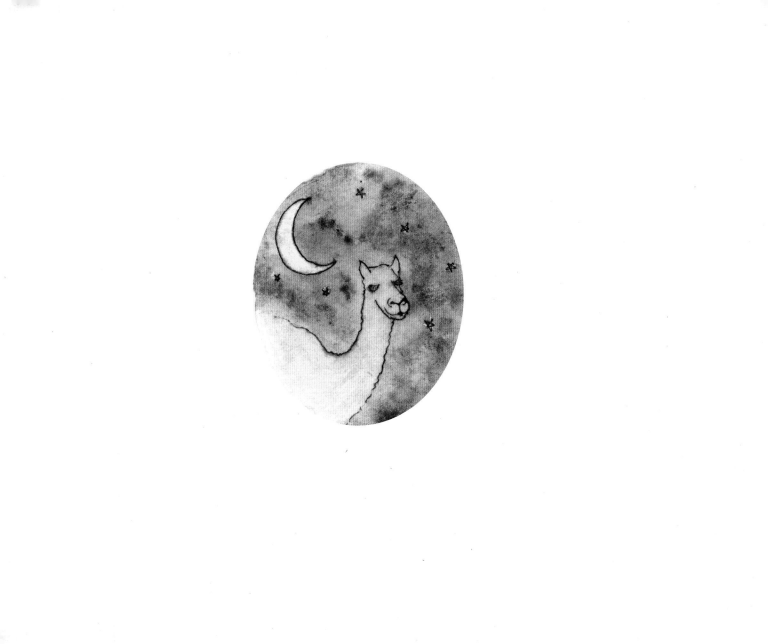

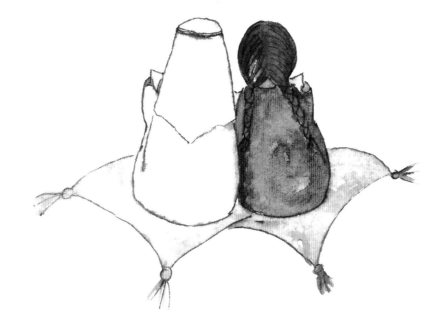

Other children's titles from
STACEY INTERNATIONAL

The Children's Encyclopaedia of Arabia
Mary Beardwood

Price: £ 19.95
ISBN: 1 900988 33X

Elvis the Camel
Barbara Devine
Illustrated by Patricia Al Fakhri

Price: £ 9.50
ISBN: 1 900988 399

Fizza the Flamingo
Marilyn Sheffield
Illustrated by Patricia Al Fakhri

Price: £ 4.50
ISBN: 1 900988 631

A is for Arabia
Julia Johnson
Illustrated by Emily Styles

Price: £ 8.50
ISBN: 1 900988 550

The Pearl Diver
Julia Johnson
Illustrated by Patricia Al Fakhri

Price: £ 9.99
ISBN: 1 900988 585

The Cheetah's Tale
Julia Johnson
Illustrated by Susan Keeble

Price: £12.50
ISBN: 1 900988 879

A Gift of the Sands
Julia Johnson
Illustrated by Emily Styles

Price: £12.50
ISBN: 1 900988 917